PETIE THE PARROT'S AMAZING ADVENTURE

AS TOLD BY BROWNEE THE STORY LIZARD
Book 1 in the Brownee the Story Lizard Series

Written by Sharon Lee Brown and Illustrated By Sharon Revell

MJ Brown

Special thanks to Angela Criser

-S.L.B.

For information regarding permission, write to Sharon Lee Brown c/o Starla Enterprises, Inc.

Attention: Permissions Department
9415 E. Harry St., Ste. 603, Wichita, KS 67207

ISBN: 978-1535182690

Mr. and Mrs. Smith were on vacation in Honduras. They found me, a baby lizard, all alone on the side of the road. I have a short leg and a big tail.

No problem going home to Kansas in Mr. Smith's pocket.

The children were thrilled. They took good care of me and started feeding me fruits and vegetables with the bugs. I grew very fast. They named me Brownee, for the unusual brown spots on my nose.

I listened to the parents tell stories and read to the children to teach them to be good, kind, and polite. I thought someday I wanted to tell stories to children and I did.

I made my voice soft and nice like Mrs. Smith's. "Yes, I can talk."

A teacher heard me reading and asked if I would read for the school children. I agreed.

The hall leading to the auditorium was long and my tail bumped into a wet floor sign. I knew I was a bit clumsy and off balance, but it didn't bother me. I was happy to be myself.

The children were laughing about the noise and a talking lizard. I entered the stage, standing up about three feet tall. I started laughing with them.

"Hello, I'm Brownee, the Story Lizard. I am here to share Petie the Parrot's Amazing Adventure."

Petie is a small, greenish-yellow parrot with a broken leg. He can fly, but crashes when he lands.

It is a mystery what happened with Petie. He came from OKLAHOMA. A nice lady found him living in a basement being fed and cared for in KANSAS. She felt sad for the little guy.

She asked a man named Jim, who loved animals, if he would take him. Jim agreed and learned all he could about parrots.

Petie's cage was now in the living room with lots of light and music. He swayed back and forth with the music and loved the warm sunlight.

Jim started letting him out of his cage. He rubbed the back of Petie's neck, gave him love, attention, and delicious treats.

Sometimes Jim would put Petie in his travel cage and take him outside. Petie heard other birds and sounds. He was happy for the first time.

Jim decided to move to CALIFORNIA.

Susie the Ladybug was sitting on the yellow rose bush. She was watching Jim load the trailer and green truck, feeling sad they were leaving.

The pretty yellow rose bush had survived storms, large hail, and harsh winters. Jim came with a shovel to take the rose bush with them. He was not a fan of flowers, but this one was special.

Susie thought for a minute she would like to go with them. But she couldn't leave her family and friends. So she jumped off and cried a little. She would miss them.

Petie and Jim began the long, exciting journey. They were in a blizzard in the COLORADO mountains. They traveled into WYOMING and UTAH. They drove through the desert and more mountains across NEVADA, then finally to the new home.

Petie again lives in a bright living room with the music he loves.

He gets to go everywhere with Jim. He stays in nice hotels. He has been near the ocean and went to Yosemite Park. His journey has been amazing and he's ready for more adventures.

The yellow rose bush survived and is thriving in CALIFORNIA. The green truck is still going.

"Wow! This is a happy story," Brownee said, with a big lizard smile. "I hope you look for my next story about Susie the Ladybug.

Maybe you will help other children be good, kind, and polite."

GOOD: It is doing the right thing, following rules, and being pleasant.
KIND: It is caring about people, animals, and things. Doing nice things.
POLITE: Please, thank you, you're welcome, excuse me. Be respectful.

Made in the USA
San Bernardino, CA
18 October 2016